A Memoir

The Quest Of The Flower Pink

By

Sherley Florival

Table of Contents

This book is dedicated to you Mon
Amour~~~~~~~~~

You've awakened me, and I thank you.

Published by Absolute Author Publishing House

www.absoluteauthorpublishinghouse.com

PAPERBACK ISBN: 978-1-64953-475-0

Cover Photography : Adonai Florival

Editor: Jessie Raymond, Sherley Florival

sherleyflorival.com

Introduction

We are born into this world but we are not of it, 1 John 2:15-17. We live our lives so carelessly, yet every step and every move is orchestrated and meticulously part of a bigger plan. God, thank you for every misstep, every failure, and every roadblock. Thank you for being my divine orchestration in this place I was born to, called life. If only we let God lead us into our own individual purpose, our intricately designed path then we can become originals like the originator, as we show the earth something that has never been seen.

Chapter 1

<u>NEVER</u>

As a child, being 8 years old, I had a sense of God; I knew that He existed, but that was as far as it would go. Growing up in a Haitian home, we adapted to the culture of Catholicism, with the common rituals of christenings and baptisms. We also attended Sunday mass regularly. In my family, God was a respected figure, but that was it — just a figurehead. Yet, I always felt like there was more. I yearned and had a longing for the greater, but at the time, I just couldn't form what I was longing for into words. One day, while no one was around, I decided to go to my mother's bedroom; a large chamber with a nine-foot wooden armoire and a bed befitting the meaning of her name - Queen - that she hardly slept in. *Come to think of it, where did she sleep?* In my innocence, I kneeled to that famous portrait of the white Jesus that every household carried. I bowed my head and began to pray from my heart. In a moment of purity, I spoke these words, "J'ai envie de te reconnaître (meaning, *I want to know you*)." The image was always staring at me with those eyes, and finally, I gave in and "wanted to know Him." After my plea, as I looked up at the image one last time, I heard an internal nudge to run and never do this again. I didn't know what or who it was, but it frightened the wits out of me.

I came from a wonderful home. My father, who was a sociologist, was well-known in our society with colleagues such as the president and the prime minister at the time. I remember being very proud of where I came from, for I grew up with the Haitian elites of our society, played with their children at the lodge we attended every weekend and attended private schools managed by nuns. More so, with my mother's societal parties being second to none, I felt like where I was born into was wonderful. But as you know, all good things must be tested.

With Haiti's political and economic climate failing, my father had to make some hard decisions. In addition, our family fell on a path downward after years of blissfulness, mainly due to my father's upbringing. This warranted my mother's request for divorce later on. I would love to go into that, but no one wants to be reminded of their former sins.

My father was desperate, hearing that my mother was abroad. Not

knowing what to do in her absence, he entrusted us three - myself,

older brother, Jean-Philippe, and younger sister, Vivre - to his

niece, absolutely oblivious of what we were about to endure.

Usually, when one migrates to another country, it's in the hope of a

better life, but in my case, it wasn't. Our New York abode was no

bigger than our two-car garage back home in Haiti. Haiti's

economy was declining, and yes, it was with hope that we were in a

country where dreams come true, but it wasn't the hope I imagined.

We lived in a "third-world country" like foreigners say, but it

wasn't evident in the life we were accustomed to. Bathing myself

was unheard of; I could have drowned! We always had running

toilets — always! But within a month in the greatest country in the

world, our toilet in this grimy New York apartment was stopped.

This meant we had to use a bucket with a plastic bag over it to poop in, and had to throw it away ourselves. Yes, I said what I said!

I was also bullied at school. My sister had to save me one day by breaking my bully's arm and calling her a "motherfuckin' bitch." Well, it was no surprise she said that, seeing that she knew all the English curse words after a week on American soil. Of course, if our parents were there, I don't think we would've had this experience.

Finally, after three months - which felt like six - my mother came for us. My happiness returned to me. Although I was a daddy's girl, my alliance shifted pretty quickly. *Oh, happy day!* A mother is like a "jus citron dans une chaude journée," meaning *iced cold lemonade on a hot day*. After all that we had experienced, her presence refreshed us. It didn't matter what was to come, our mother was here.

When I was 9 years old, I gave my life to Christ. On my very first encounter, I felt like a floating bubble in a Disney movie. I felt God in the most potent manner unknown to many. This encounter was a direct response to the longing that I had three years earlier — the desire to know that God was real, and that there was a force bigger than me out there. I held on to this experience and kept it dear, allowing it to lead me as I searched for more.

A few years later, when I was 17, my life came to a halt; during this period, I was in a place of despair. I had graduated high school, but couldn't go to college because I was financially challenged and undocumented. The only choice given to me was a marriage proposal to my distant cousin for the sake of the American Dream

of US citizenship, which I refused.

That very season of despair led me to seek God for comfort and

direction. I ended up at an Apostolic Prophetic Church that gave me

the very foundation for the next level of my life. I offered my

service as a member of the ministry of helps (you know, those

women that throw clothes on ladies when their legs or derrière - or

any part of their bodies - are exposed. We didn't want unwanted

arousal at the sight of curvaceous ankles). I would get prophetic

words of prosperity, healing and how to find my niche, etc. Out of

so many words of exhortation, one prophecy stuck with me. It was

one from an older gentleman, who was very kind, and spoke

eloquently. In his words, he referred to me as a flower; a flower

being planted on a good soil to germinate, to be groomed, watered and then replanted on a different soil. Later on, I found out that the meaning of my last name was flower in Spanish. There and then, I found God in worship, and afterwards, I was taught prayer and fasting. After some time, my spiritual journey progressed to the next level. After 11 years of service, I was led to take the leap and move to San Francisco, California, in pursuit of an acting career. I had been modeling for years, and the next logical step was acting. In my years of modeling, I also acquired prophetic words about acting. Normally, I'm a shy person but I felt a consistent tug in my spirit that drew me to this area. So, when I turned 30, it seemed as though I was ready for this journey.

In San Fran "Black Hollywood " they call it, in every city, there's a set somewhere; it's only a matter of choosing the sets to be a part of, and that's what I did. I began doing extra work to make a living in between my legal temp assignments. For 3 months upon my arrival, I worked on set as an extra, and eventually, on November 7, 2011 like any other day, I was called to come in. After my morning ritual of dropping my son at preschool, and praying that the set would be wrapped before 6pm to avoid the late fees, I arrived on set, parked and asked for directions. As I got there, things were moving pretty quickly. We were shooting in a boutique, and I was told to stand on the sidewalk and get checked by the wardrobe person.

As I stood there, a black SUV that drove by with a figure in the back seat stood out to me. In 5 minutes, they called myself and two other actresses in. I went in and sat on a box, waiting for the rest of the crew to come in. And then, in walked Bravehart — one hell of a man! He was tall and big; he had a powerful, yet, shy presence.

Despite his intimidating stature, he had the purest eyes I have ever set my eyes on; those eyes, though, innocent and timid, spoke truth. They drew me in and were compelled to go skinny-dipping in that sea of onyx.

He sat not too far from me and made a joke, which everyone - but me - laughed about. Honestly, he was talking so fast I didn't understand what was said, so I couldn't even get the joke. I just didn't get it. He wasn't funny to me at all. Earlier, as I walked in, I didn't know that I would like him and be attracted to him, but I was, easily, effortlessly; I had finally found my type.

I managed to get through the interior scenes, and now we were shooting the exterior of the boutique. While the crew was setting up, I was asked to stand in the camera frame. We locked eyes, and what happened next, I could never have prepared for, nor imagined;

what happened next would never have even entered my consciousness. In a moment of absolute stillness, in a street full of onlookers, and crew working all around us, it seemed as though it was just the two of us in a plane or dimension unbeknownst to everyone within this 9-mile radius. I felt my inner self; my spirit, a woman, a fairy, Tefnut, awakened. As I stood there, I could feel her moving in and out of me to get a glimpse of him — Bravehart, that is. Immediately he looked back, she hid herself inside me. She was beautiful, and was now awakened after a period of dormancy. As she looked at him and hid herself, so did I. And at that very moment, we became one entity. I was no longer leading, as we were both aware of each other now. I became her, and she became me. We knew him, and even loved him profusely. This revelation caused us to hide ourselves, for our secret was revealed, thus causing us to be bashful.

While in the boutique, I looked at him, liked him and found him physically attractive. But when I saw him through her eyes, I loved him. There, I saw his purity and realized I loved him long before we actually met in person. Someway, somehow, he knew it too. There even was a possibility that he called me to him; that he needed me, and then I arrived.

Bravehart stood there, next to the camera with eyes and mouth wide open staring, gazing at my every move. To this day, I don't know what he saw. *Did he see her too? What was his encounter?* From that kairos moment, I have NEVER been the same. He awakened me. It was divine timing and purpose colliding; meaning, I was on the right path, and what took place and what was to come was my life's purpose, my ministry, my destiny. It was a spiritual

phenomenon. After this encounter between us, we were given an

option to either wrap up or stay for the next location. It was the

perfect day I had hoped for, so I wrapped up early. Meanwhile, I

was curious as to what would have unraveled if I had stayed.

Now, back to real life. In the coming months until 2012, I was on a

temporary, one-year long legal assignment with a Buckhead law

firm. The extra work was getting redundant; although, within those

few months, I managed to get my SAG eligibility. I needed

stability, consistent income and a set time to pick up my little

chatterbox.

In the weeks that followed, I could not stop thinking about him. I

thought about him so much, my head would spin; I would feel my

thoughts going a million miles per hour. It was yet another spiritual phenomenon. Then the severe headaches began. I knew they weren't natural. Something spiritual was happening to me that I could not decipher, and it caused me to be frustrated. In my frustration, I asked God, "Is he my husband?" And the very next day, I had a dream...

Chapter 2

ENOUGH

Bravehart stood there, washing his car; it was a nice car. I stood

there, watching him in front of a shed that looked like a huge dog

house like in "Clifford The Big Red Dog." As I stood there, he said

to me, "I'll be back in June, will you be here?" In the dream, I

knew we were fast approaching the end of April, and June wasn't

too far away, but I didn't respond. I said nothing. It was a casual

beautiful sunny day in the dream — nothing special. But internally,

we were burning with romance.

What we felt for each other was from the third heavens. The

romantic tension between us was a fiery unquenchable fury. We

loved each other intensely, and it burned within us; although it wasn't physical, but spiritual, it affected us physically. We were in love with each other, and our presence was all that mattered. Physical touch wasn't even the focus; to us, being together was ENOUGH. He didn't love me more than I loved him, I didn't love him more than he loved me; we loved each other equally.

Now, I remember something that happened to me as a little girl - when I was about 9 years old - living with my Tati, and going to this small endearing Baptist church. Being my first introduction into Christ, I was sitting at a table with a sweet white woman, who may have been my Sunday school teacher. She had me repeat after her the prayer of salvation, with eyes clenched, and a French accent. I whispered, "Jesus please come into my life..." As soon as the prayer ended, within seconds, I felt an unquenched amount of joy. I blurted out, "I feel so much joy Mrs. Woolbright." And in excitement, she cried to me that it was Christ in my heart. I was so full, that it was all I could speak of for the next two days. My first experience was immense; it engulfed me. My emotions were on high drive.

As I woke up from my dream of Bravehart, I knew that my encounter was similar to my very first encounter with Christ. It is said that when you have a spiritual encounter with God, your senses are not hindered by the flesh; they are heightened to capacity, therefore, you feel everything in its purest form. My love for him was so intense, it engulfed me. It was nothing like I had ever felt before; for, and to any other human being. This was when it occurred to me that he wasn't just another mundane individual; he was my spirit equal to my twin flame, and the answer to my question to God the night before — my husband. Biblically, we're all familiar with the book of Genesis, which speaks of Adam being

formed out of the dust of the ground, and Eve being made from one

of his ribs, meaning that at one point, they were one entity.

This was quite similar to Heliopolitan theology, also known as

Egyptian mythology, which speaks of Shu, who was the Egyptian

god of the air and supporter of the sky. He had a wife, also known

as his companion, Tefnut, who was the goddess of moisture, water

and fertility, created by a god Atum Ra, their father. This theory is

called the split soul theory, which states that humans originated in

pairs, bound in one body, with one original soul, but were split in

two, for doing something offensive to the gods, after which the

newly separated humans forever wandered the earth in search of

their long-lost soulmate, to become one again.

Goethe, a German thinker, in his novella, employed Plato's split soul theory, which states that soulmates are destined for each other; each have head-aches on the opposite sides of their heads, because they used to be conjoined at the back, and originally had one brain. WHAT! If this was not an explanation to those nasty, heart-wrenching headaches I had been experiencing, then I didn't know what was. I was dumbfounded! Having this spiritual encounter was enough - I mean, if you would have felt what I felt in that dream, you would agree also - but to have some type of humanistic interpretation of what was happening to me was an extra sense of hope that I wasn't berserk.

In the coming months, life continued — meeting deadlines at work, church, etc. The redundancy of paralegal work was draining, but it paid me well enough for the time being. One day, in between bankruptcy filings, I picked up my phone, and began clicking away until I saw a post about a business seminar. *Guess who was a speaker?* This event was to take place on the 13th of that month. Prior to that moment, I had found out all his details through social media; his birthday, birth place, etc., and in the course of my little investigation, I found that we were both born on the 13th; of course, that could not be a coincidence. *Was he trying to send me a message? Did God speak to him as well?* My heart was racing with excitement, all the while I was trying to purchase those tickets that sold out within 20 minutes of the post. Obviously, I was disappointed, but I knew that something was happening, and that kept me going.

Two days later, at about 3 in the morning, I woke up, feeling sick. I vomited, cleaned myself up and went back to sleep. As I slept, I dreamt of a message from Twitter, giving me instructions on what

to do next. It said something like this, "Tuesday, I want you to…

Wednesday… etc." As I scrolled down to see who it was from, it

said, "Braintart."

For years, my dream state was a conundrum; chaotic was an

understatement. I could not comprehend them, nor could I interpret

them. I also couldn't remember them in detail. My dreams would

go from one sequence to the other, and some were repetitive. It was

something I couldn't fully comprehend, so I left it in God's hands.

At some point, I was told by a dear friend to write them down, and

ultimately, I would make sense of them later on; so I did, and I have

not stopped since.

Since my encounter with Braveheart, my thoughts and dreams have

gone from chaos to clarity; I now remember every detail, every emotion, and also, in some cases, the interpretation thereof. Dreaming about the same person twice was a phenomenon, but the other dreams were a wonder.

San Fran is a small city, and the entertainment industry is even smaller. As an actress, you're likely to run into other actors - on auditions, sets and networking events - so I knew I would run into him one way or the other. The entire time, I was anxious, as to if he felt the same way like I did, so, for the following weeks, I tried to book as many jobs as I could, hoping to see him again. After several attempts, we ended up on the same set.

Anticipating that we would reconnect and share our encounters with each other, drifting off into the sunset, I looked at him, and he at me, but nothing. He ignored me the whole time, and didn't even utter a word. I went back home, confused, thinking, *what if I conjured all this mentally?* Because what I felt spiritually/internally wasn't lining up with what was in front of me — the natural. I thought that *I was such a fool to have believed that he loved me too, and this was nothing but the devil!* Time passed, and I lived my life. I still saw him in different places, and although we never spoke, there was something between us that was undeniable. I was in a state of belief, yet, in a state of doubt; there was an internal conflict between my spirit and the physical world. I forced myself to focus on my career and moving to the next level... and then I had yet another dream.

My third dream of him began like this; my pastor, his sister and I, were in a big house. My pastor was on the other side of the room, on a table, with his back against us. The house was empty, except for a few couches and that table. I was talking to his sister, and when I was done, I went over and around the couch where he sat. I sat down and tried to kiss and caress him but he was unresponsive and turned away, saying, "I can't! I can't!" First, I thought maybe it was because he had a girlfriend in the dream, but then, he began praying to God in front of me, oblivious of the fact that I was still there. He said, "Lord, help me to allow someone to love me."

As soon as I woke, I began praying for him; I had never prayed for him before. I then spoke to God, saying, "You've just put his heart in my hands; you've trusted me with his deepest heart cry. Why have you done this?" I then began to feel how deep this relationship was before it actually even began.

Months and months went by, and I tried to stay focused. By this time, my legal assignment had ended, and they picked the temps they wanted to keep with an offer of a raise of a dollar more, which

I declined. The breaks between temp assignments were liberating. It meant that I could work on my craft, full throttle. My son was getting older, and I had a backup plan in case I couldn't pick him up. My routine was good, and it kept me going. By fall, I started working as a paralegal again, with a much higher pay than I was offered previously. At this time, I hadn't seen him since spring, and my frustration dwindled.

One day, I saw his Facebook post, congratulating his friend and his wife on their marriage. It made me smile, for now I knew God was dealing with him too. I was also ready - ready to love him and be there for him without any reservations - for I learned that he had a hard childhood and had overcome way too much. I wanted to give him something he never experienced; give him a better ending for the horrible beginning he had to deal with, growing up.

Over the years, it didn't matter who I dated, I would always ask God if said person was to be my husband. It didn't matter if I was into him or not, nor if it was the first or the 6th date. There's nothing as pointless as doing purposeless things. Our time on earth is precious, so, knowing from my soul each time, if a particular journey was of God was priceless to me. And the entire time, God never responded until I asked about Bravehart.

A few months passed, and I hadn't heard from him, nor had I seen him. On a nice Sunday afternoon, at about 2pm, being fully awake, I heard a voice call my name, "Sherley." It wasn't an audible voice; it was from within, and it definitely startled the hell out of me. It was like what I would hear people with spiritual encounters say. They would usually speak of hearing a voice out of nowhere, warning them of something. It was as though my gift was evolving, and I welcomed the evolution.

In that moment, I panicked because someone could be in danger, and I had no idea who could it be. So, my first instinct was to call my father, but there was no answer. Then I really began to worry. I worried because my father had been talking about death for years, and prepared my siblings and I for his passing, with letters year after year of his will and testament that would change as with his mood. I think he removed my brother Jean-Philippe at some point, only to add him right back. I called him again and found that he was fine. Then I thought to myself, my father would never call me "Sherley." He would only call me by the French pronunciation of my name, "Cherlay."

I pondered, and then figured that this had to be him — Bravehart, that is. And I was right. I found out that he was gonna be on a particular set, and was ready to meet. So, I responded to the email, and got approval to come. I was on set the following day, and was ready for our love journey to begin. As I arrived on set, we had each other's full attention. He looked so nervous. First, he wore a hat, then later on, I saw him remove it while he brushed his waves. We were both so shy that each of us was waiting on the other person to make the first move, and we both missed our moment. Looking back, there were different chances we both missed out on to speak with each other, because we allowed fear to hinder us. I told myself, "The next chance I get, I'm gonna take it." *More love, less fear,* was my nouveau motto.

Chapter 3

YOU SON OF GOD

Bonne année , *Happy new year*. Scientists have said that we dream every night. I'm sure there's some truth to this theory, but I believe I only remember the dreams that matter to my spiritual evolution. My next dream was very faint; he wrote to me and said he was coming for me early in February. The dreams were still unexpected, but became more common. I didn't know what to think of them, and I also had to discern if they were from God, The Devil, or me. It was year 3 after our initial meet, and I was already getting tired of waiting. I knew without a shadow of a doubt that there was something between us but, I could not understand why we were still apart after what we both experienced. Our connection was out of this world, and no matter how many times I thought about quitting, I couldn't, for I felt a deep steadfast feeling of pledge to him. It didn't matter how much time passed between us, even without the physicality, I always felt him with me. Trying to be with someone else was pointless; it meant I would have to have another encounter that was greater than my encounter with Bravehart. It was agony, and I don't remember telling God that I signed up for this.

Another part of a dream came a month or two later. He wrote to me via email or Twitter - I don't remember which - with a questionable phrase. This dream was similar to the dream I had a year earlier, with the common denominator being Twitter. I decided that if I were to get another chance to see him, this time, I would find an opportunity to speak to him. In the last chapter, I spoke of Bravehart calling my name. At the time, I didn't realize that it was a form of telepathy. He called me and I heard him; these revelations were both a gift and a curse.

Ready to make up for the time lost, and in eagerness to see what all this dreaming and headaches meant, I was pressed to at least have a conversation with him. I saw him on set again, and as usual, he was ignoring me. On this day, I wasn't having it, so I courageously approached him from behind, tapped his shoulder and introduced myself, knowing that we both missed our chance last time. Bravehart looked at me and yelled, saying, "YOU CAME FROM ALL THE WAY OVER THERE TO TELL ME THAT! Well, hi to you too!" And with that, he walked away.

I was appalled, so much so that I grabbed my pink sweater and ran out of there with an adrenaline rush. *Why was he so angry?* We hardly knew each other. *Is this how you treat someone you love?*

Did I deserve to be humiliated in front of everyone? What an ASS!

He was the one who was too afraid to approach me.

"Take responsibility for your shortcomings as I have!" I said out loud on my drive home. Once I got home, I reflected on what happened. His reaction was so bizarre. I later began to understand that although we didn't officially have a proper introduction, he was way past that point, and was angry that I was pretending like we weren't. So, I went back to my dreams, and there was the Twitter dream that I had twice. It was then I figured out how to communicate to him. So, I managed to lock my page and give him and him only access to it. I then began to talk. I told him everything that had happened to me thus far. He was so happy. I was happy too, but it lasted for like a nanosecond. I spilled my guts, and he just listened without any response, or very few responses. I would ask when we could go on dates, and he wouldn't answer. He was

satisfied with the way things were, and I wasn't, so I stopped

writing. During those years it was, "I'm coming for you," but he

never came. Well, deep down, I knew that he would because I kept

dreaming. I was just so frustrated with what was taking so long, and

not knowing the reason for deliberately staying away. It had been 3

years already, and I was tired. I also felt terribly lonely. I was

walking in a place of spirituality that I had never been — at my

apex. You could have called me a prophet if you wanted to. But

then I couldn't share my ordeal with anyone; people would've

thought that I was crazy. I remember briefly sharing with a

co-worker friend of mine that I felt like Bravehart was my husband,

and she practically cursed me out. She told me I was delusional and

living in a fantasy. Could I blame her? She was right. I thought I was crazy many times, how much more an outsider. We all have our different purposes, and they're as unique as our fingertips. Our journey is ours and can't be shared with anyone else, although we desperately want someone tangible to share it with. I was being elevated beyond my peers, and only isolation could get me to where my purpose hid.

I didn't speak to Bravehart for weeks. My next dream was in early spring of that year. We were on a stage in front of a large crowd. He asked me to come up as his significant other and have me address the crowd. While I was speaking, he kissed me on my shoulder. *It was a nice dream, but it will never happen,* I concluded. Yet, with all this debacle, I was still clinging to hope. I thought one of the reasons why we weren't a regular couple was because he wanted me to remain private - owing to his public status - but this dream led me to believe that we would finally be public yet, still maintain our privacy. Although I was exhausted from this fictitious relationship, I would go into my shell and regroup. I continually told myself that all that I was going through was not wasted; that it was building something internally that I could not see. *For I reckon that the sufferings of this present time are not worthy to be compared with the glory which shall be revealed in us,* Romans 8:18. I knew God was in it, with everything in me, but what I did not want to be was another Christian woman who believed God for their husbands blindly, forgetting about themselves without keeping these men accountable, and allowing them to become their Lord based on a word from God, before their love was tried and proven. When I couldn't go another day of physically being without him, I told him that I would rather be alone, and broke up with him. I needed those breaks. It's important I emphasize on the fact that it is

critical that you do what is necessary for you in your journey, in

order to remain sane on your road to Damascus, or else this stuff

will have you baker acted. So, what did I do? I traveled. I went to

my country of origin, Haiti. I spent a month in paradise. I walked

everywhere, climbed mountains, ate and gained no weight. I danced

and drank for hours. As long as you stay true to God and yourself,

it's all part of the bigger plan.

I kid you not, those breaks were exhilarating. I traveled, partied,

and focused on me, instead of what he wasn't doing. Once my

paradigm shifted, waiting for him became a lot more bearable. I

discovered that everything that I was going through had everything

to do with me and him indirectly. That became my "AHA" moment.

Yes, we live in a tangible world, by natural means, but it is ruled by

the unseen — the spiritual. It's never about others or what they do
to you, but about your response to becoming who you've been
ordained to be; others are just mere vessels used for your
expansion, for the glory of YOU, A SON OF GOD.

It was halfway through the year, and I had yet another dream. We
were in a house, it was just me and him, and he wasn't in a good
mood. He said casually that I could have the house, and my
reaction was indifferent, for I was tickled that he gave me the
house, yet, concerned that we weren't gonna live in it together. I
was pleased, because there would be no reason why this would not
happen, but life continued. Although trying not to focus on him
helped tremendously, the circumstances of life got to me. I was
renting an apartment and times were hard, and now, I had just
dreamt that he gave me a house; I actually really wanted it. It could

not solve all my problems, but at least 50% of it. I wanted the

house; I needed it. By now, my dating woes began. I debated the

continuity of dating, but I thought to myself, *how can I date other*

people knowing that he is my husband? For years, I asked God to

reveal who my husband was, and now, to reject it was like slapping

God in the face. I knew for the time being that it would be a waste

of time and energy, so I kept to myself and tried to focus on my

acting career. I learned that it's okay to be dubious, as it was my

humanity surfacing, so I did whatever felt right, in order to get

through to the next season.

During this particular period, I would have dreams within dreams. I

felt mentally unstable. I would dream of the walls moving in my

room and different spirits in my curtains; I would blink in the

dream and it would just rearrange the same thing. I would wake, but I would still be dreaming. That particular night, I had to pray to actually wake up in reality from the dream. I had had demonic dreams before, but this beat them all. I'm not sure where these dreams stemmed from at that time, but it wasn't the norm, and I wasn't sure what God was trying to convey to me. Your journey is tailor-made to who you are and where you are going. Your journey in God should not mirror anyone else, for you are an original, not a copy. Therefore, do what is required for you and your journey to get where He needs you to be.

Chapter 4

NOT SO HAPPY NEW YEAR

I'm pregnant. I was pregnant, and *it wasn't for my fictitious husband,* a friend of mine who I had the courage to confide in said. She basically cursed me and told me how stupid I was to believe this man was my husband. But of course, my belly was revealed in a dream in a Sunday afternoon nap. In the dream, I was okay with it, but in real life, I was opposed.

I wanted to have a daughter, from a marital union. It had been my desire for years. I knew what I wanted, and having a daughter was not far fetched, but with whom, was my worry. *What was God trying to tell me? Was this dream a warning to beware? Or was it a premonition like the other dreams?* Only time will tell, but I became even more cautious and aware.

August flew by and ushered in September — his birthday month. I celebrated his birthday the best way I could, buying gifts now going on year 4, waiting for the day that I would finally give them to him. Work continued and I was bored out of my mind, knowing deep inside that I wasn't fulfilled vocationally. As I was going through these motions, I got word that they were laying off the Legal department at that location. Prayer answered? Yes, and no, but thank God I had a severance and went back to acting in between jobs.

Running into him again would not be ideal, as I had not forgotten how he embarrassed me in chapter 3. But in this industry, you are bound to run into lovers, frenemies, exes, etc. I accepted an extra job, well aware of his attendance. I was booked, looking so fly and get to the gate, but guess what? I was banned from entering the premises, and was asked to leave. *Was he really behind this? What kind of power did he have over there?* It was way too coincidental, and I was so certain it was him. The insult to injury was too much to deal with, so I went home and wept like a baby. I was broken in four. I was done! With festivities around the corner, I focused on that, spent time with family and soon, the year would be over. Happy New Year! Or NOT SO HAPPY NEW YEAR, for what I endured just a couple months ago could have not prepared me for what this year had in store. I was over it… well not him, yet. I didn't tweet to him and focused on my craft. I just couldn't break my own heart over and over, so I stayed away. Well, at least I tried to. I began dreaming more frequently. My next dream was me sitting on his lap in a restaurant, and him actually listening to my

advice. Then came another dream of me being proposed to by

someone other than him. Then came a dream about an invention,

then another about a party that I was a part of. It was him there, and

us having a conversation. We enjoyed each other's company, and in

the dream, I learned that he was willing to listen and be attentive to

my needs.

It didn't last too long, because it didn't matter how many dreams I

had, how many times I saw him and felt how much he loved me

and cared for me in the dream, because in reality, he was the

opposite. He chose himself over me. His betrayal over the years

was insufferable, so much so that I questioned if God actually

existed. *Were these dreams really a spiritual encounter?* I could have sworn with my own life, that I knew God spoke through

dreams, but after 6 years, nothing aligned. He was still a brute, and

used me to occupy his loneliness. Maybe this was my cross to bear!

But I thought I'd already bore it with The Doma.

If I didn't think this was God, I would have never ever let it go on

this far. I remember asking God, "If this isn't you, close the door."

That prayer always worked every time, *but what happened this time*

around? Was my spirituality so far gone that I could not see the

signs? I don't know, and we may never know. For the first time in

my life, I lost my faith.

You would think that with my decline in spirituality, I would at

least stop dreaming, but no. It just kept going and going. I wanted it

to stop because at this point, I was so tired of them. Growing up in

an Apostolic Prophetic church, we habitually prayed prayers of divine revelations, prophetic dreams and secrets of the unknown. I manifested a fraction of those prayers, and now, they were suffocating.

I didn't know if it was God trying to encourage me or me encouraging myself with a dream of 92 wedding guests, with my father and godmother present. Honestly, I didn't care for these things until this dream.

On this day, I was bombarded with giving up, going back to Miami, just mentally exhausted from all that had happened. It was a rainy day. I took a nap, and saw the word *Talia*. I woke up and asked, "Is that my daughter's name?" It was funny because I always wanted my daughter's name to begin with an A. Well, I didn't ponder on it any longer, until months later.

There's another theory that I have learned called the dual soul, by Ricardo Sagehorn and Cornelia Mroseck. This theory was much more suited to our situation, since so much time had passed between us. It states that you and your dual never come together, but also never separate. If God was cruel, this statement would be the reason why. *Are you kidding? Do you mean to tell me the only one that my heart desires, not just on a physical, but spiritual and astronomical level, who I am connected to and feel every single day of my life, and I are not meant to be together? How could this be? This life is really meant to break you.* I read on, and thank God there was a solution. Hallelujah! There was. Any bit of hope, I would welcome with open arms. The book goes on to state that eventually, the duals live a fulfilling life together, but in order for this to take place, the Chaser (me) and the Runner (him) upon meeting are bound to a loop that once formed, is hard to escape.

Although the souls are bound together, individual growth must take

place for the duals to coexist. The transformation of maturation is

extremely painful because they are a union of opposites coming

together as a whole. The authors state that the very first connection

is a single look in the eye. Looking back, I realized this was

Bravehart and I. It states that it is like a lock and key model, where

this person unlocks certain parts of you that you knew not of.

Bravehart awakened me. I recognized him instantly. It was almost

like I knew him before I became aware of my own existence. He

was my abode. There's an irresistible magnetism from knowing

them deeply inside. Now, you can't live without them anymore, and

you're forced to come closer, since you think about each other

constantly. You feel like you've been bewitched.

Chapter 5

<u>HAITIAN MOTHER</u>

Going through a motionless life, living like a zombie from The Walking Dead, a speck of lumière surfaces. Dreams are our connection to the spiritual realms; it reveals to us the hidden mysteries of life that cannot be interpreted in the natural world, so it is vital that we lay hold of all it has to offer, for it can change our lives in a snap of a finger.

Since then, I quit my job at a bankruptcy firm, which was paying me way less than my experience had to offer. I could have been the managing attorney there with all the knowledge I brought to the table. From a place of depression, I decided on a trip to Miami, in search of my mother's comfort. It didn't matter how old I was, she cared for me as if I was still 6 years old. She would bring me breakfast in bed, a Haitian breakfast with boiled plantain, egg omelette, with tomatoes, a dash of Maggi sprinkled with spinach and a side of avocado. A Haitian breakfast is not truly complete unless there's a side of jus chadèque or jus citron (Grapefruit or Lemon juice). She bathed me, scrubbed my back and even washed my punani (*vagina*) hair with vigor. C'est ma mère, la Reine de notre famille (meaning *she's my mom, the Queen of our family*). I got there just in time for my niece's birth. I was in the hospital room when she was born, only to discover that her parents agreed to name her - yeah, you guessed right - Talia. Yes, TALIA. She was born in August of that year, and I had the dream in January of that same year. Coincidence? Nope, absolutely not, zilch, nada! I was in total shock. It blew me away because it was totally unexpected, and it also meant that my dreams really do come true. I had so many

dreams that I didn't see come to fruition that I stopped paying

attention. I felt okay, until this upcoming news.

In addition to my niece being born, someone else was to be born.

Yes, as I mentioned before in my dream, I was pregnant, but in

reality, guess who else was pregnant? Bravehart's ex-girlfriend,

Adra. When I saw the pictures, I shook uncontrollably for three

minutes. Nothing prepared me for this. I couldn't believe it, but it

was true. I remember my pastor telling us the story of how she met

her husband, and how she knew he was hers and how she waited

for him even through engagements with two other women. I said to

myself I would never go through this, but look at me now. I pleaded

with God to take this pain away and to tell me that it was a joke.

My heart was bleeding out, and out with it was ma joie de vie (meaning, *my joy of living*). My faith was already hanging in the balance, but now, I had lost myself too. Ma mère couldn't understand what was happening to me. If you know anything about HAITIAN MOTHERS, you would know having her see and experience my disheveled state was absolutely maddening for her. She pleaded with me by my bedside every day to tell her what was wrong with me, but as much as I wanted to tell her everything, I just couldn't even find the words.

We take things so lightly, without a second thought. Most of us have a will and desire for different things, but what happens once that is taken away?

My desire to eat was something I never thought twice about, but during those times, the desire to eat escaped me. I was never hungry; the will to eat nor the craving for food was there. I was never hungry. If I ate something, it was for my mother's sake, and the ability to get out of bed to even wash myself was draining. My frame was fragile from all the weight I lost. We both suffered so much that she had me hospitalized. I spent two months in a therapeutic program meant for those diagnosed with acute depression, which usually affects women of 60 years of age and older, in my 33rd year of life.

During those months, my prayers were pleas and whispers, asking God to help me go back to who I was — to the confident sexy woman I was. As much as I wanted to be back there, I couldn't, for the motivation to get better for myself was absent; but in place of that, my mother's love and the subsequent dream was my motivation to get better.

On one fateful Saturday, at midday, I was feeling a little uneasy

after eating. As I laid there, trying to find a good position to get

comfortable, I drifted away in a stupor, dreaming...

I saw myself by this old mall that my friends and I used to frequent

during lunch time and after school. It was absolutely perfect

because I would use my lunch money to shop, and I always went to

school looking cute. Anyway, as I stood there, I looked across the

street and I saw a man with a little girl in his arms; he was

molesting her. In utter panic, I screamed at him, "What are you

doing?" My shrills sent him running like a demon when Christ

would show up. As I crossed the street looking for the little girl,

who seemed to disappear out of thin air, I noticed that I had my son

on one hip and Bravehart's newborn son on the other. I was

petrified and so protective of their safety after what I just saw that I felt an overwhelming sense of love for not just my own son, but his son as well. I loved them equally. They were both mine without distinction. Again, the emotion, in its potency like my very first dream of our romantic love but replaced by a mother's love on steroids. I loved them so much, and there was no difference between them, as they were both my offspring. I knew it, and felt it. I woke up from this dream, just like an actor in a movie; abruptly, upright and speechless. "God is literally trying to kill me!" I said. "I will not condone his behavior!" But immediately I was reminded that his behavior had nothing to do with the child. Like in times past, my reality was unmatched to my dreams, but I knew it was a supernatural encounter that had just happened to me, and there was no way I could do this in the flesh. I needed God every step of the way. I didn't see this child but I loved him so deeply. He wasn't mine, but yet he was. Him and my son were equals, just like

Bravehart and I were.

Chapter 6

NEGRO PLEASE

One day, after years of souffrance (meaning *suffering*), I awoke, and every hurt and pain that was done to me by him, was broken. It didn't hurt anymore. It has been said that when God puts you in a situation, He is responsible for you. Anything that happens, he has orchestrated; therefore, the restoration is His responsibility as well. And for me, it was just that. I went to bed one way and woke up another. We roam around the earth sometimes in a lifeless state and have no idea how to get back to who we were or walk towards the new version of ourselves, like souls lost in purgatory. I realized that I was just existing, and when God healed me, He breathed life back into me.

My bones were alive and my heart was revived. *But, was it over? Did my healing mean that my purpose thus far was finished? Would these headaches finally release me?* Maybe God had a council, and the council decided that I should go through these things for the purpose of this book. I don't know. What I do know is that although I was healed, I still loved him. And even if I decided I was done, how could I remove him from within me. I could still feel him, as he was a part of me. When he was bothered or stressed, so was I, and it was even difficult to function in the mundane. We pursue each other in the daylight, and surrender to each other at dawn. During these instances, he began to naturally draw closer after all these years. In the past, I would feel him close to me spiritually. First, it began with him watching me sleep, and then it progressed to him running his fingers down my leg as I slept, to him putting his hand over my mouth, softly. In all these instances, I was never afraid because his spirit was kind. When it's demonic, it's immediately evident.

Now, he had figured out where I lived and was showing up at my apartment complex out of nowhere. But he was still not communicating; it was my headaches that did the talking. I knew he was near based on the throbs and variations of the headaches. I would see him at building eight, pretending to make a phone call; meanwhile, I lived in building seven. He would follow my route to work. He knew my schedule. I would pull out of the parking garage at work, and there he was, on the other side of the street. I would be driving on the highway and he would pull up in front of me. What he was trying to prove or say, I had no idea, and I was tired of trying to figure it all out. He did all of this, and still never approached me, so, I let it be; I let him do whatever he wanted and I just lived. Ma Vie (meaning: *my life*) was returned to me, and I intended to live the best out of it.

I'll deflect a little to give a word of advice. My message to you, reading this book, is that you must live your life. Don't just have dreams and aspirations, but set goals to realize them. Do whatever your heart desires. Expose yourself to what your heart yearns for, so you won't be fooled or used when someone offers it to you. You can't be tempted with something you've already experienced. If you desire money, give it to your damn self, so, the fool won't tempt you to sell your soul for it. Men use trips, gifts, etc., to get you to remain complacent. Don't be a foolish virgin.

Now, back to my story. By this time, he had yet to spend any time with me, but he had offered me money, college funds for my son, a house, a car and movie roles, just for me to continue to put up with

his bullshit. It had been a few years since we had consistent

communication between us. He was losing his grip and he knew it.

I loved him like I loved myself but I would not, and I could not

settle for the bits and pieces he was offering. I wanted more.

Although, at times, I didn't feel like I deserved more, but grace

allotted me more, and I stood on that fact. I knew what I wanted,

and if he wasn't going to give it to me, I would give it to myself. In

every culture imaginable, a woman has been a conquest by men, so,

when did this change? Just because he was my soul flame didn't

mean that he would automatically get a pass. His love still had to be

proven and tried. Many women accept men for the pawns that they

are and never challenge them to elevate to kings. Why would you, a

deity, marry anything less than who you are? This is not Greek mythology, we're not giving up our heavenly selves for mere humans, by no means! We must do better. This goes for men as well. Relationships are designed for the evolution of self. So many of us are living lives that are stagnant, not producing a thing, just accepting whatever comes our way.

I found out later, that Bravehart, knowing his power, was meticulous on how he wanted his life, and the role I or anyone else would play in it. He wanted to give me my purpose, but I didn't care if it was a good or great plan, no one was giving me my purpose; it would either come from God or me. BROTHER PLEASE, Allé Chita! (*Go sit down*) My next dream was me in the middle of Time Square, looking at a fancy written card stock invitation with a date of November 6, 2016 on it. I thought to myself in the dream, *this must be my wedding date*, but I was later disappointed because the date didn't represent us. We share 6 ,9 and

13. The only link was that this date was the day before we met.

I had the courage to believe in us once more and moved back to

San Francisco, hoping that we were going to be married the

following year. And guess what happened? Nothing. I had grown

accustomed to being let down by him, so, this was the beginning of

the end.

Chapter 7

<u>THIRTY-8</u>

Thankfully, my next dream was about me. I saw myself looking back at me and I was happy with all smiles, as if I saw my own reflection. I had never dreamt about myself alone, and I didn't know what it meant, but I knew it was good. At that point in my life, although I was in pursuit of acting, I felt like something was missing. I liked it, but I didn't love it. I was evolving.

The industry had a lot to offer, but as something else other than an actress. I was working on set on a continuous basis, as I booked a stand-in gig for about 4 seasons of a show, and it was monumental, especially since my jobs were never consistent. I knew my schedule as far in advance as they could render, and I could still take my vacays unhindered; life was good. I was on the next level of dating.

I had gone from talking to people to now actually saying yes to going out on dates. They were necessary for the time being. I felt butterflies again. I felt flirty and sexy. I was admired and cared for, and boy did it feel great! In addition to that, I was eating well. I was still dreaming about him, but I didn't give it much thought because this was probably the 35th dream of nothingness and pettiness! My father lives in Montréal and I visit him every chance I get. This time, I decided to go, and of course, I had a blast. I went to the nursing home where he resided and spent all day with him, hearing the stories of his friendships, past flings, and lovers before meeting my mother. Arguments and debacles with the other residents featured in his story. He also told me stories of his younger self, our name of Spanish origin, meaning *flower*, and his studies in Paris, Louisiana, Florida and California that led him to his PhD. I loved them all. There's so much to learn from our elders, and what they

say remains with us forever. Traveling is my escape; a necessary

luxury that is priceless.

Upon returning home, after the shenanigans, I felt uneasy; not the

regular uneasiness that comes with going back through the work

and school routines, but so much deeper. I was in between

resurrection and death. This book title that I wrote down years ago

kept resurfacing in my thoughts within the space of three days. It

just kept on coming back up, and after the internal turmoil and

struggle, I realized that writing was my next voyage; after all, it

was my escape through it all. I wrote everything that I had gone

through for the past 9 years and had no idea what it would bring or

what was to come. So, at 38, I discovered that I'm a writer. I was

shouting it from the top of a mountain, and from the core of my being, "It's my outlet, my release, my calling." I believe writing all that happened to me was a form of healing for me, and also a means of absolute preparation for this book.

Every year, I would do a study on the age I would be turning, trying to get an idea of what was to come. 38's biblical meanings included: your calling, life's work, and labor. This discovery led to a place of such contentment, for I knew that my time was not delayed. I was in alignment with destiny, and all that I endured was divinely orchestrated.

We must live a balanced life. Being able to find your life's work, the ground you're meant to toil is as equally satisfying as fighting a mate. Both were needed for me to feel fulfillment, but maybe not all at the same time, and that's quite fine.

I've done all sorts of different jobs, from cleaning, to waitressing, modeling, paralegal work, acting, even landscaping, to finally reaching this resting place of a writer. Everything that I have done has led me here, and it's glorious.

Amidst the toil, trials, and testament, I realized that life is never about the other person or the circumstances you're in, it's all about your own development of becoming your true self. The vices that we go through are just layers in need of unfolding. With that mindset, a lot of suffering can be avoided, and in times of enlightenment, or a change in perspective, it has been avoided. Now that I knew where I fit into and came to terms with who I was, it was time to discover the type of writer I was. As I thought of this, I didn't have to look far because my passion was my journey, my experiences and my spiritual encounters. I just knew that my first book would be about Bravehart, for my whole wilderness experience had been about our lives woven together based on one dream.

Throughout this whole ordeal, I want to mention what I call "moments of tenderness." The human experience can somewhat be an awful experience at times, but as awful as it gets, it's also wonderful and beautiful. My first moment of tenderness was on a still night, in between non-REM and REM sleep. I felt Bravehart watching me sleep. Now, I'm not quite sure what to make of it, because it wasn't a dream; I felt him. His demeanor - which was very gentle - and his sweetness were pulling me. I have had experiences before with the spirit of men that would visit me in the witching hours, but their intentions were evil, and they desired me so intensely that it felt like forceable violence, so much so that I would wake up, calling on the name of Jesus for help. But he was gentle — not a speck of evil nearby. This was the first of many. Every encounter after that had a common thread — tenderness. In the warmth of the day, in between a dream and a reverie, when life was so silent that you could hear crickets stridulating, he searched for me spiritually and he was found by my bedside, watching me sleep, or stroking my thigh. All these kairos moments that we share are unforgettable, and are ours to cherish.

Chapter 8

STRANGER I RECOGNIZE

It's amazing how God works. Like I said earlier, I suffered with these debilitating headaches. They would get really horrible too. It all began in the fall of 2011, right after we met. I had this mind-boggling, intense headache that lasted for a month straight. At the time, I couldn't figure out what was happening to me, nor did I know the connection thereof. Year two rolled by, and it continued, this time more intense. Other times, it was a mild discomfort, but as time progressed, it worsened to the point where I was unable to function in doing mundane things.

Fast forward to year nine, I noticed Bravehart drawing a bit closer. And as long as he heard, saw, and knew what I was up to, the headaches were moderate. I realized that Plato's split soul theory was at work. If you can remember, this theory states that each soul

has headaches on the opposite sides of their heads, because they

used to be conjoined at the back, and originally had one brain.

Many times, I prayed for these headaches to go away; if this theory

served true, he was also experiencing some sort of pain as well.

When we were unaware of each other, life was sweet and painless,

but once we knew the other person existed, separation was agony

until we communicated on a plane (I was never really totally

satisfied) that we were both content with. In most cases, there's a

spiritually dominant person, that is more intuitive, whereas, the

other party is more logical, practical. When we were in harmony –

well, what we called harmony at that time - I suffered no

headaches. But when he was stressed about me, I felt it, and I

would often ask, "What's wrong with you? How can I make you

feel better?" Sometimes, we would solve the problem and the headaches would subside, but the dramatic difference came when he began to see me in everyday life, like we were a couple, and knew what I was up to. I'll tell you how this played out another time.

After year 9, I discovered that in previous years, his stress came from not seeing me or knowing what I was doing, despite that I talked to him every day. When he began to know my daily routine, my whereabouts and what I was doing inside my home, he was at ease. So damn nosy! There are so many questions I have about this experience that need answering, and honestly, I've made peace with the fact that I may never get all the answers. Here we are two souls who love each other deeply, intensely, yet, cannot find a common ground still, after all these years. I didn't know him, yet, I loved him. I had never spoken to him, but I knew the language of his heart. What we share is inexplicable. As much as there were times I wanted to forget him - as he can be quite toxic at times - I couldn't. He was in my head and near me. His eyes were always watching me. It was almost as if he was a part of me, and as you know, you can't get rid of a member of your own body, no matter how useless it may seem.

In the light of the COVID-19 virus, one of the senses that is attacked is our sense of smell. Who knew your sense of smell was connected to your taste buds? People who contracted the Corona Virus couldn't smell or taste; abilities that were necessary for everyday life. Some people just can't be forgotten no matter how hard you try. You can't outrun them by running into the arms of another. I don't know what happened to us that day we met - I didn't know stuff like this happened or even existed - but I love him deeply still. 9 years after, and it was still full of passion, although we never actually touched.

I woke up one day in such agony, realizing that there was a chance that we may not actually end up together, despite the callings, the witness in my spirit and the dreams I had. This realization broke me. *With all that we had been through, how could we not be? What was the purpose thereof?* My logic tried to justify that it was to birth this book; to bring out the writer in me. But deep down, my soul felt robbed; it wasn't sufficient. Me becoming a writer wasn't enough; I wanted him also, as I loved him too much. I wasn't ready to let go. We, even after nine years, still never began our journey together. Everything was just open, without any closure, without a heart-to-heart conversation; it was just left to interpretation. We were at a standstill. I had done enough, and he had no idea how to make amends, so I left him, finally, for good. It was no longer up to us; our hands were tied. It was now up to God to restore the years and birth us together. It was time for us to live apart and in solitude with God's help and hope of bringing us into oneness.

As my father smiled while looking through the family photo album, he couldn't help but notice a baby photo of our family he had never seen before. Thankfully, I labeled all of the photos just in case, for his eyesight was not what they used to be. For years, he raved about his research and how they meant everything to him, just to come to a place of old age where he couldn't read nor even write like the scholar he was; his eyesight diminished after multiple cataract surgeries in the right eye. As he looked closely at one particular photo, he couldn't recognize anyone but one person. It was a teenage girl holding a baby along with a young man who was about twelve to fourteen years old. He thought, *I've seen this young lady before but I don't remember where.* While in deep thought, a nurse knocked on the door for his daily check up. As he attended to the nurse, he lost his train of thought.

A month later, he died in his sleep. But before his demise, one day, as he slept, he figured out that the baby in this foreign picture was the daughter of an old flame he met back in his early 30's, while studying anthropology at Louisiana State University, and the young man next to her was her firstborn, who was also my father's child. This child was included in his final will and testament, which was updated seven days before his passing.

As the attorney sat and told the family this tale, my blood boiled

with anger. I was sitting there, fumed, thinking he might as well

have left him my inheritance too. *How could he?* After all these

years, not one time did he mention to our family that we had an

older sibling — not one time! I was furious, and couldn't not funnel

my emotions properly. My siblings of course had a different

reaction; one was amazed, while the other was indifferent, for both

of them were too busy with their lives to even attempt to figure out

what became of this young man. It was all left up to me to figure

out who this person was, and honestly, curiosity killed the cat. I

wish I was as nonchalant as my siblings, but I wanted to know - I

had to know - so my search for this long-lost brother began…

Chapter 9

AWAKENED

Being part of an Apostolic Prophetic church for years, I experienced so many phenomena. One being my dream state, which at the time was absolutely chaotic. After some counseling, I was encouraged to write them down. It didn't matter how crazy or bizarre they were, writing them down was ideal, and praying for the interpretation thereof was encouraged.

For years, my dreams were so weird that even with all the teachings about the 3rd heavens and the anointing that I experienced every Tuesday and Sunday, I still couldn't understand them. But when I met Bravehart, something in me surfaced. My true self was made alive — AWAKENED. It was so apparent from the beginning, that

I missed speaking of how crucial this moment was. He awakened the spiritual part of me that laid dormant. No one else was able to, but him. For this, I'm grateful, and know that he is the part of me that has been lost and now is found.

I urge anyone who met their soulmate, soul flame, your reflection at an opportune time; do not take it lightly. No matter how painful it is, explore it, digest it, and jump in head first, for it truly is a phenomenon. Absolutely nothing will make sense, but life is about the inexplicable, bizarre moments we encounter, that change our psyche for the better. Nonetheless, we must live a balanced life, not allowing ourselves to be "too heavenly minded and with no earthly good," like the scripture says; likewise, we shouldn't be so practical that we miss the moments of magic in our lives. I was in such a state of euphoria that I missed the practicalities of life. As I turned

29, my wisdom tooth came in. Initially, I didn't think much of them, for they hurt occasionally. But as time progressed, the pain grew worse, and honestly, I didn't want to remove them, so I endured for ten years. At 39, I could no longer take it, I had to remove them. As soon as I did, not one headache. They were gone, I mean gone. I swear to God that I was certain that these heart-wrenching debilitating headaches were connected to Bravehart; I swore I felt him. I swore that there was a connection. This mind can convince you of anything; anything, do you hear me! What a fool am I, face-palm emoji, face-palm emoji!

Finally, after ten years, the dots began to connect. I honestly didn't think that some certain unending questions would be answered, but they began to unravel one by one when the time was right.

I thought, "Now that my headache is gone can I dream about someone that I can actually be with physically. Are you there, God? It's me Margaret."

Bravehart and I were in a suburban neighborhood, walking on the sidewalk, not following very closely. He was ahead of me, and I, behind him. I watched him speak to someone to my left while I looked to my right and saw a family friend in a hurry into her spacious car. By this time, he crossed the street to the right and motioned with his long fingers to come to him. As I crossed the street and followed him, I entered a home which I knew instantly was his mother's. As I saw the living area to the left, I mentioned out loud, "Wow, what a spacious room!" I then followed him in, and around the home, something to my left caught my attention. Distracted by what I saw, my focus shifted, and I forgot that I was supposed to follow him. Meanwhile, he was walking to the kitchen and opened the refrigerator. By this time, I was catching up, and soon, I was standing by the refrigerator door. He opened the door and handed me a flower; a flower with dark pink and light pink petals.

"Eat it!" he said, with an assertive tone.

Huh! I looked at him, puzzled, but he was serious as can be. His tone was firm, as if he stepped into himself. I was hesitant to eat the flower, pondering whether it was an edible flower or not. It sure as hell didn't look edible, but I relented, and with a yucky look on my face, I took a bite. As I began to chew, I couldn't tell if it tasted yummy or not. After all, it was a flower. I continued to chew and swallowed, thinking to myself, *his mom made this; this must be special to him.* With this thought, I took a second bite and bit into a heart-shaped piece of meat inside.

As soon as I woke, I thought*, he's gonna give me this house; he bought me a house.* So, I focused on the house until one day, it was all clear. He gave me his heart. His heart was not only given to me by God, but now, he willingly handed me his heart.

Over time, we both had become different versions of ourselves. Although I loved him deeply, I was always unsure of fully committing to him. He, on the other hand, grew bold and courageous. In my very first dream, he asked me a question, which I didn't respond to. It was, "Will you be here?" And I felt like in my first dream, this very question was left open, but once in this final dream, he was no longer asking me questions; instead, he took control and answered them for me. Look at the phrases "Will you be here?" in relation to "Eat it!" Both phrases were coming from

two different people in the span of a decade. I also realized that I

needed him to take charge. Leaving it up to me would make me

hesitant and run for the hills because hid mode of operation was so

unconventional to me.

Chapter 10

<u>I FORGAVE</u>

We finally arrived at our 10th year of being together tumultuously, although we weren't together like a normal couple; I still wasn't communicating with him at all, and he was still around, watching me. November of that year would make it our tenth, and guess what? No change, no big reveal — nothing. *Was it really worth the wait?* With all that happened between us - the pitfalls, the mountain tops, encounters and revelations - all of it was supposed to end like a Disney movie with love and a lifetime of happiness at the very end, but it ended like a Edgar Allen Poe book, with the raven echoing, "Nevermore, Nevermore."

In the 10th year, I realized a couple of things, one being that

although he loved me, he could not allow my love to penetrate his

heart. There was a dormant part of him that desired this relationship

but relented and he couldn't trust me because his guards were a

shell that kept everyone out. I never stood a chance, because

although he wanted to believe that I was different, the expectations

and the standard that I was held to was impossible to live up to. He

wanted absolute loyalty without being held to the same standard,

and when I fell short, his disdain was apparent. I was labeled a

whore, for he could not believe how I could be faithful and loyal to

someone who had been given nothing, and continued to believe and

try again and again.

Eventually, I left him, again, which proved his motto that no one

could be trusted. It didn't matter what I did, I always missed the mark, for he was looking for perfection. It was like in the old days where the First Lady stood by her husband no matter how much he embarrassed her, abused her or his indiscretions. That was the definition of love to him. His distrust for people ran deep, and I, the woman that loved him, couldn't pray it away or do anything to help him, for he didn't even allow me to enter.

With this realization I cried, until my eyes turned red. All of a sudden, everything made sense; his treatment and our conversations. All the ill things he did to me was a revelation of his hardened heart. His actions were without shame or apology; every single time, it never failed. He laughed and joked about my suffering, he tormented me with others, and my agony seemed to bring him joy. Spiritually he was good but in reality he was malignant, and lacked maturation.

With all that took place, that same year, I had another awakening.

In my years on this earth, I had never experienced trauma so severe

that I questioned if God existed, but this time, I did. He took God

away from me. In turn, I was angry at God, and could not

comprehend that this person was God-sent.

After months of vexation, I FORGAVE him. Once I did, I loved

him even more. My love for him was now unconditional. It didn't

matter what he did or didn't do, or his intention; none of it

mattered. I loved him with all his faults; this realization opened me

up and made me fall in love with life for the first time. I told

myself, "You must endure this. Let the ridicule and pain transform

you," and that I did. I loved him deeply, so I was willing to do

anything within my power to make us work. So, I pursued. If he

was gonna be there, I was there, every time, despite that he rejected me. In one or two instances, he would have his security escort me out. I remember coming home after the first time it happened and balling, trying to decipher if this is the person I was made for; his rejection was demeaning and so hurtful. You do not treat those you love this way.

Yet, with every rejection, it got easier until I was no longer phased by his response. I did as Paul; I chastised my body and brought it under servitude. The results it yielded was immense towards my spiritual evolution. After a season of endurance, I made sure that I did all I could and exhausted my efforts to be with him, so I wouldn't live in regret. Eventually, I became satisfied, therefore, looking back wasn't part of the equation. I left the ball in his court because after all was said and done, his rejection fortified me, while he became more crippled and fearful.

It is said that God numbers our tears. With every tear drop that fell, it fell toward his detriment. This explains why women move forward, evolve and heal while men remain the same. Who would've thought my tears were working for me and still at the same time working towards his demise? Everything is two-fold; action to a reaction, good versus evil, an antagonist to a protagonist. You cannot sow evil and intend to reap goodness, you will reap what you have sown. Our story was not going to end like a Disney movie, but I was now okay with that. Whatever force that drove us together, was the same force that unveiled it all.

Chapter 11

BRAVEHART

September, with its fallen leaves and the crisp air of Autumn hitting your face, has always been a month of the ending of transition for me. In September, I either close a chapter or open a new one. And this would mostly happen in the evening of the twenty-second or the morning of the twenty-third; this was where this took place. I found some photographs and letters with origins of importance and gave it to him. I toiled and toiled to get them, and he, in his despair and sadness, refused them. Dealing with his past was something that he wasn't ready to face. But why his reaction was so bizarre was that he loved talking about his past.

I looked at the photographs myself and couldn't make any connection. As he walked away, with his shoulders slung over yet still, his 6'6-foot frame towering over shelves, cabinets, basically everything in the basement, I followed him, in an effort to touch him and provide comfort. His strides were so big due to the length of his legs, so it took me a good minute to catch up. Once I finally arrived, I put my hand on the small of his back and rested my forehead on his brawny frame. It's polarizing, having someone you deeply love and care for, yet, not be able to help them overcome painful traumatic experiences from their past. It is said that when going through trauma children, do not have the language to articulate what happened to them, but what about adults? Most times, the words cannot form, just a lump in the chest that sits there, dying to be liberated, but still remains.

He turned around slowly and embraced me, not knowing what to do next. As we stood in the middle of the room, I looked up at him. Looking into his eyes was my Achilles heel. They were always pure, and spoke with veracity. Looking at them reminded me of how much I adored him and was willing to do anything to make the ending of his days filled with happiness. With that thought, I grabbed his enormous hand. In the days of old, kissing of the hand was a sign of adoration. So, in that very instance, with eyes shut, I finessed with kisses the dorsal side of his hand, expressing respect, love, and fidelity with each peck, and took a quick gaze to see if he was intrigued; he was delighted and surprised. With his eyes widened and an open mouth, I turned to his palm and whispered with kisses, "We are married, just without ceremony, yet."

This was a constant fantasy. His hands made me so happy, I loved

them. They were so enormous. I wanted to rub them all over my

body, fondling myself with them, biting them and doing it all. They

were my fetish! Falling asleep after this rêverie was hard, yet, I

managed a dream of us three — myself, Adra and Bravehart.

I stood alone in front of a home, which looked like a house built for

a theatrical play, with different rooms with furnishings but opened

for the audience to see. I stood there, frightened, because inside the

house was calm but outside the home, there was chaos and danger

all around me. I remember seeing rising waves coming toward me,

yet, not being able to touch me. In almost every dream that I had

dreamt of in this manner, whatever danger I faced never touched me; it would come close, but it never prevailed to harm. I was there, just watching the havoc with a visage of worry.

Bravehart and Adra walked into a room in the home. She said, "Look," pointing at me. Then he ran to me, frightened, in a bid to save me. When he approached me, he grabbed my hand, kissed me on the lips and helds me close as we watched the chaos all around us. After this, she disappeared and was nowhere in sight.

As this happened in the dream, I'm floored with happiness. We could finally be one. This man I had been waiting to see was finally here! I felt like a black floating Mary Poppins. I felt like Jesus; instead of walking on water, I was skipping on it! We could finally stand side-by-side and conquer the world. He was my dream lover. It was then that I thought that the kiss felt like I was kissing my brother.

In conclusion, Bravehart was a conduit for the greatest spiritual transformation of my life. It was the most painful relationship that I had ever encountered. He alone with all his imperfections was worth every heartbreak, every tear. He is my foe, my frenemy, and the love of my life, but the journey that I thought or the expectation of the relationship we would be in was not the end of it all. Who I became through it all is bigger than the result of us being together. Go through what you're meant to go through, don't run from any pain, take it in, let it be a force to transform your very being, for this is one of the tools used to transmute you to a different plane. In addition to this, know that people are a vessel for transformation. It is all about you. You are mastering yourself, becoming a conqueror over your thoughts, emotions and life. Life is meant to be lived and experienced on every level. When it comes to love, true unconditional love that is, it's not what is being said in

mainstream media. You have to love the person without restriction,

and this begins with love for thyself first.

I have died so many times in the course of this relationship, and I'm

grateful for it. This was my truth and my thorn.